A Book of Months

TEDD ARNOLD

Dial Books for Young Readers  New York

Dedicated to Gerry Schultz whose work was the seed from which an idea grew, and to my wife Carol who nurtured, weeded, trimmed, loved, and brought this book to fruition.

Acknowledgments

Many hands pulled miles and miles of thread through what seemed to be acres of cloth to produce this book. My heartfelt thanks to all who gave of their time and kept me in stitches:

Ursula M. Paccone
Pam Grant
Carol Arnold
Pat Batulis
Geraldine Schultz
Theodosia R. Schultz
Debra Haldeman
Vicki I. Bennett
Frances Padgett
Judy Clark
Nancy A. Doman
Victoria Rounds
Debbie A. Jacobus
Sharon J. Newman
Ruth Elizabeth Bruning
Lisa Hilliard
Laura L. Palmer
Cathy Clark Harrell
Kay Leininger
Margaret Brennan
Reges J. Bush
Bob Schultz
Patricia M. Bottcher
Mary Jane Buchanan
Carolyn S. Winslow
Nancy H. Paddock
Mary Jane Rolls
Marcia H. Robinson
Cheri A. McElroy
Debbie Reynolds
Pat Reimsnyder
Jennifer T. Long
Deborah M. Spezialetti
Denise K. Hagan
Jackie Yacubic
Maria D. Russ
Mary E. Hildreth
Kelly Pickering
Sandra A. Clemons
Susan H. Arnold
Netti Caporiccio
Marie K. Dale
Janet I. Pierotti
Anne E. Marshall
Judith D. Gulick
Jane Sugawara
Eileen Warren
Ann-Marie Allaire
Eileen N. Hogan
W. Richard Hamlin, Ph.D.
Susannah K. Murphy
Debra L. Arnold

I'd also like to thank Peter Elek for his unflagging professional support and personal friendship.

Special thanks to Our House Fabric and Gifts, Elmira, New York.

And a tip of the hat to Linda Peterson.

Grateful acknowledgment to Betty Ring for providing a photograph of a sampler from her collection.

Grateful acknowledgment to The Pilgrim Society, Plymouth, Massachusetts, for providing a photograph of a sampler from their collection. Photographer: Alan Harvey.

Border linen courtesy of International Linen, New York, New York.

Publisher: Phyllis J. Fogelman
Editor: Toby Sherry
Art Director: Atha Tehon
Designer: Nancy R. Leo
Production Director: Shari Lichtner
Photographer: Lee A. Melen, Northlight Photographic Studios, Ithaca, New York.

Published by Dial Books for Young Readers
A Division of Penguin Books USA Inc.
375 Hudson Street
New York, New York 10014

Printed in the U.S.A.
First Edition
W
10 9 8 7 6 5 4 3 2 1

Library of Congress Cataloging in Publication Data

Arnold, Tedd. Mother Goose's words of wit and wisdom:
a book of months / Tedd Arnold.—1st ed.
p. cm.
Summary: A collection of Mother Goose rhymes
centered around the months of the year.
ISBN 0-8037-0825-4. ISBN 0-8037-0826-2 (lib. bdg.)
1. Nursery rhymes. 2. Children's poetry.
[1. Months—Poetry. 2. Nursery rhymes.] I. Title.
PZ8.3.A647Mo 1990 398′ .8—dc20 90-30334 CIP AC

My melodies will never die,
While mothers sing and
babies cry.
M. GOOSE

January brings the snow,
Makes our feet and fingers glow.

The north wind doth blow,
And we shall have snow,
And what will the poor robin do then?
Poor thing.

He'll sit in a barn,
And keep himself warm,
And hide his head under his wing,
Poor thing.

Whether it's cold, or whether it's hot,
There's going to be weather, whether or not.

The greedy man
Is he who sits
And bites bits
Out of plates,

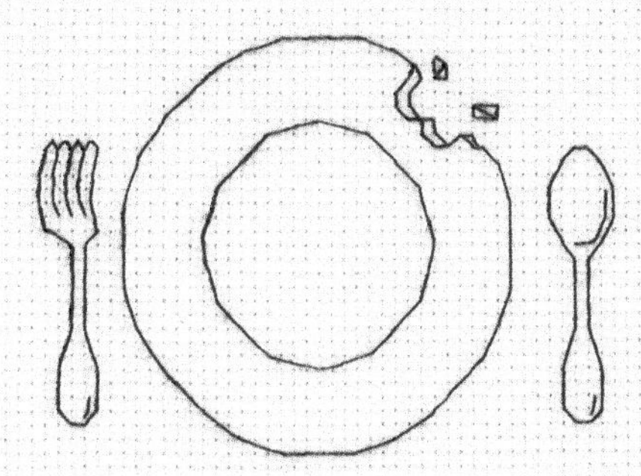

Or else takes up
An almanac
And gobbles
All the dates.

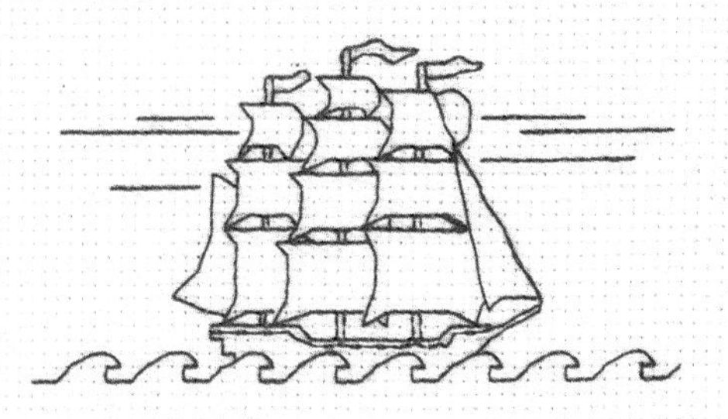

I saw three ships come sailing by,
Come sailing by, come sailing by,
I saw three ships come sailing by,
On New Year's Day in the morning.

And what do you think was in them then,
Was in them then, was in them then?
And what do you think was in them then?
On New Year's Day in the morning?

Three pretty girls were in them then,
Were in them then, were in them then,
Three pretty girls were in them then,
On New Year's Day in the morning.

One could whistle, and one could sing,
And one could play the violin;
Such joy there was at my wedding,
On New Year's Day in the morning.

How many days has my baby to play?
Saturday, Sunday, Monday,
Tuesday, Wednesday, Thursday, Friday,
Saturday, Sunday, Monday.

February brings the rain,
Thaws the frozen lake again.

Lavender blue and rosemary green,
When I am king, you shall be queen.

ABCDEFGH
IJK LMNO PQR
STUV WXYZ
The rose is red,
The violet is blue,
The honey is sweet,
And so are you.

Yankee Doodle went to town,
Riding on a pony.
Stuck a feather in his hat
And called it macaroni.

When Jack's a very good boy,
He shall have cakes and custard;
But when he does nothing but cry,
He shall have nothing but mustard.

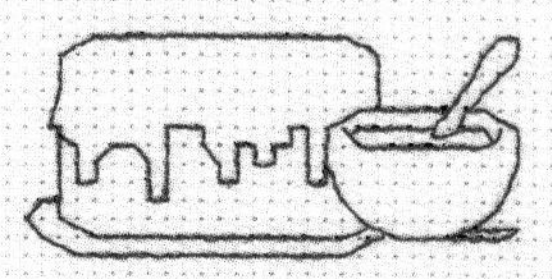

Hey diddle, diddle, the cat and the fiddle,
The cow jumped over the moon.
The little dog laughed to see such sport
And the dish ran away with the spoon.

March brings breezes, loud and shrill,
To stir the dancing daffodil.

One leaf for fame, one leaf for wealth,
One for a faithful lover,
And one leaf to bring glorious health,
Are all in a four-leaf clover.

Sing a song of sixpence,
A pocket full of rye;
Four and twenty blackbirds
Baked in a pie.

When the pie was opened,
The birds began to sing;
Was not that a dainty dish
To set before the king?

There was a crooked man, and he walked a crooked mile,
He found a crooked sixpence against a crooked stile;
He bought a crooked cat, which caught a crooked mouse,
And they all lived together in a little crooked house.

See a pin and pick it up,
All the day you'll have good luck;
See a pin and let it lay,
Bad luck you'll have all the day.

Daffy-down-dilly has
come to town
In a yellow petticoat
and a green gown.

April brings the primrose sweet,
Scatters daisies at our feet.

I bought a dozen new-laid eggs,
Of good old farmer Dickens;
I hobbled home upon two legs,
And found them full of chickens.

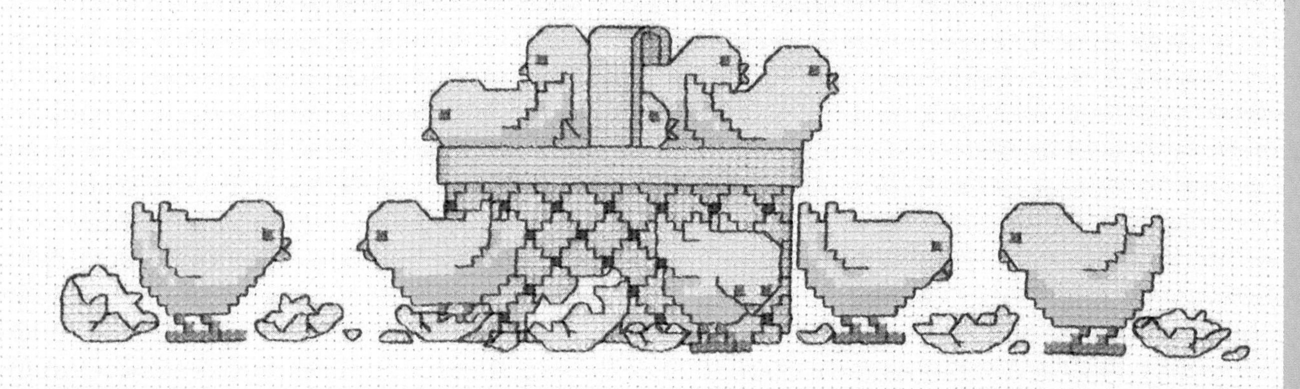

Rain, rain, go away,
Come again another day.

Baby and I
Were baked in a pie,
The gravy was wonderful hot.
We had nothing to pay
To the baker that day,
And so we crept out of the pot.

Cackle, cackle, Mother Goose,
Have you any feathers loose?
Truly have I, pretty fellow,
Half enough to fill a pillow.
Here are quills, take one or two,
And down to make a bed for you.

1
2
BUCKLE·MY·SHOE
3
4
SHUT·THE·DOOR
5
6
PICK·UP·STICKS
7
8
LAY·THEM·STRAIGHT
9
10
BIG·FAT·HEN

May brings flocks of pretty lambs,
Skipping by their fleecy dams.

One, he loves; two, he loves;
Three, he loves, they say;
Four, he loves with all his heart;
Five, he casts away.
Six, he loves; seven, she loves;
Eight, they both love.
Nine, he comes; ten, he tarries;
Eleven, he courts; twelve, he marries.

March winds and April showers
Bring forth May flowers.

The cock crows in the morn
To tell us to rise,
And he that lies late
Will never be wise;
For early to bed
And early to rise
Is the way to be healthy
And wealthy and wise.

Pat-a-cake, pat-a-cake, baker's man,
Bake me a cake as fast as you can;
Pat it and prick it and mark it with a B,
And put it in the oven for Baby and me.

The fair maid who, the first of May,
Goes to the fields at break of day,
And bathes in dew from the hawthorn tree
Will ever after handsome be.

June brings tulips, lilies, roses,
Fills the children's hands with posies.

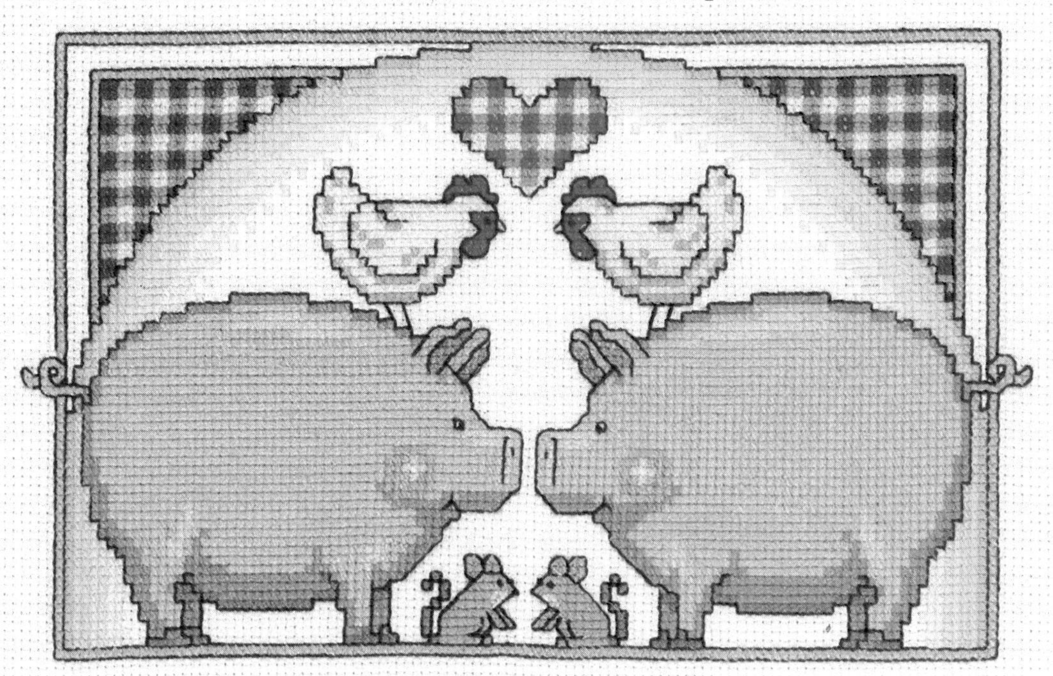

Birds of a feather flock together,
So will pigs and swine;
Rats and mice will have their choice,
And so will I have mine.

ABCDEFGHIJK
LMNOPQ
RSTUVWXYZ
Hearts, like doors, will ope' with ease
To very, very little keys,
And don't forget that two of these
Are "I thank you" and "If you please."

Good, better, best; never rest
Till Good be Better and Better, Best.

Jenny Wren last week was wed,
And built her nest in Grandpa's shed;
Look next week and you shall see
Two little eggs, and maybe three.

MARY MARY QUITE CONTRARY
HOW DOES YOUR GARDEN GROW?
WITH SILVER BELLS AND COCKLE SHELLS
AND PRETTY MAIDS ALL IN A ROW.

WINTER'S
SLIPPY, DRIPPY,
NIPPY.

SPRING IS
SHOWERY,
FLOWERY,
BOWERY.

SUMMER'S
HOPPY,
CROPPY,
POPPY.

AUTUMN'S
WHEEZY,
BREEZY,
SNEEZY.
ABC

Hot July brings cooling showers,
Apricots, and gillyflowers.

Little drops of water,
Little grains of sand,
Make the mighty ocean
And the pleasant land.

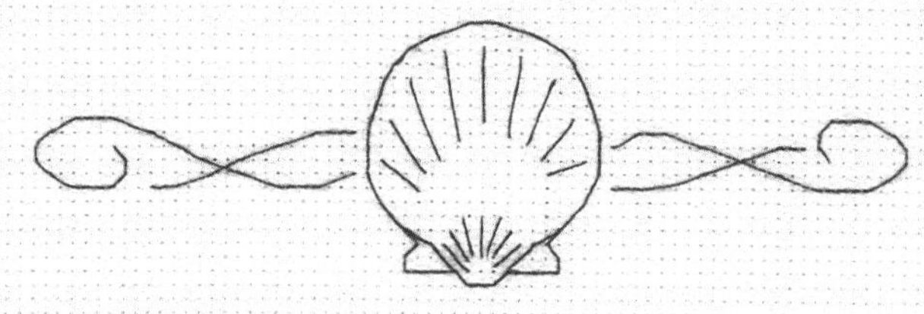

I like little pussy,
Her coat is so warm,
And if I don't hurt her,
She'll do me no harm.

So I'll not pull her tail,
Nor drive her away,
But pussy and I
Very gently will play.

Pussycat, pussycat, where have you been?
I've been to London to look at the queen.
Pussycat, pussycat, what did you there?
I frightened a little mouse under her chair.

There was once a fish. (What more could you wish?)
He lived in the sea. (Where else would he be?)
He was caught on a line. (Whose line if not mine?)
So I brought him to you. (What else should I do?)

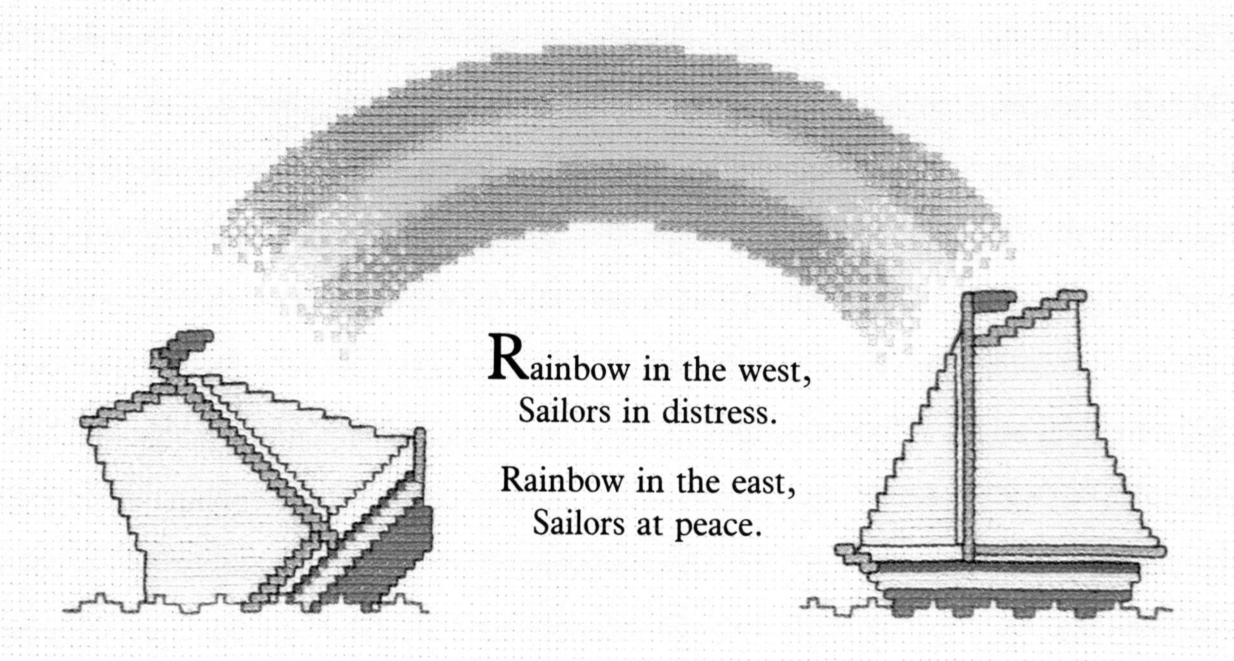

Rainbow in the west,
Sailors in distress.

Rainbow in the east,
Sailors at peace.

Jack and Jill went up the hill,
To fetch a pail of water;
Jack fell down and broke his crown,
And Jill came tumbling after.

August brings the sheaves of corn,
Then the harvest home is borne.

All work and no play makes Jack a dull boy,
All play and no work makes Jack a mere toy.

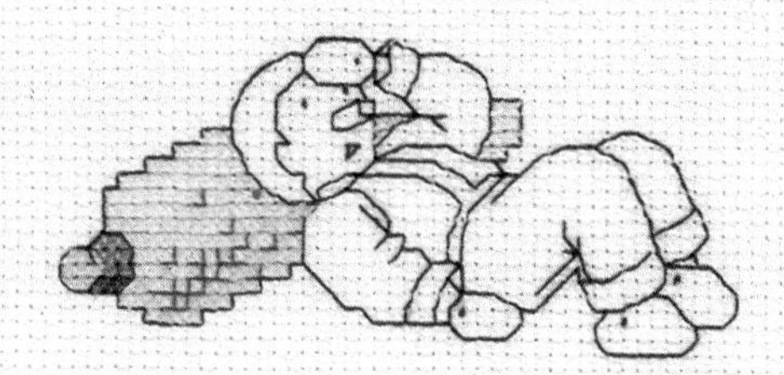

If you are to be a gentleman,
As I suppose you'll be,
You'll neither laugh nor smile,
For a tickling of the knee.

Calico pie, the little birds fly
Down to the calico tree.
Their wings were blue
And they sang "Tilly-loo"
Till away they all flew,
And they never came back to me.

Charley Warley had a cow,
Black and white around the brow;
Open the gate and let her go through,
Charley Warley's old cow.

Sleep, baby, sleep,
Thy father guards the sheep,
Thy mother shakes the dreamland tree,
And from it fall sweet dreams for thee,
Sleep, baby, sleep.

September offers breezes soft
Until the fruit is in the loft.

There's a neat little clock,
In the schoolroom it stands,
And it points to the time
With its two little hands.

And may we, like the clock,
Keep a face clean and bright,
With hands ever ready
To do what is right.

had a little
Its fleece was white as
And everywhere that went
The was sure to go.
It followed her to one day,
was against the
It made the laugh and play
To see a at

Monday's child is fair of face,
Tuesday's child is full of grace,
Wednesday's child is full of woe,
Thursday's child has far to go,
Friday's child is loving and giving,
Saturday's child works hard for his living,
And the child that is born on the Sabbath day
Is bonny and blithe, and good and gay.

I had a little hobby horse
And it was dapple gray,
Its head was made of pea-straw,
Its tail was made of hay.

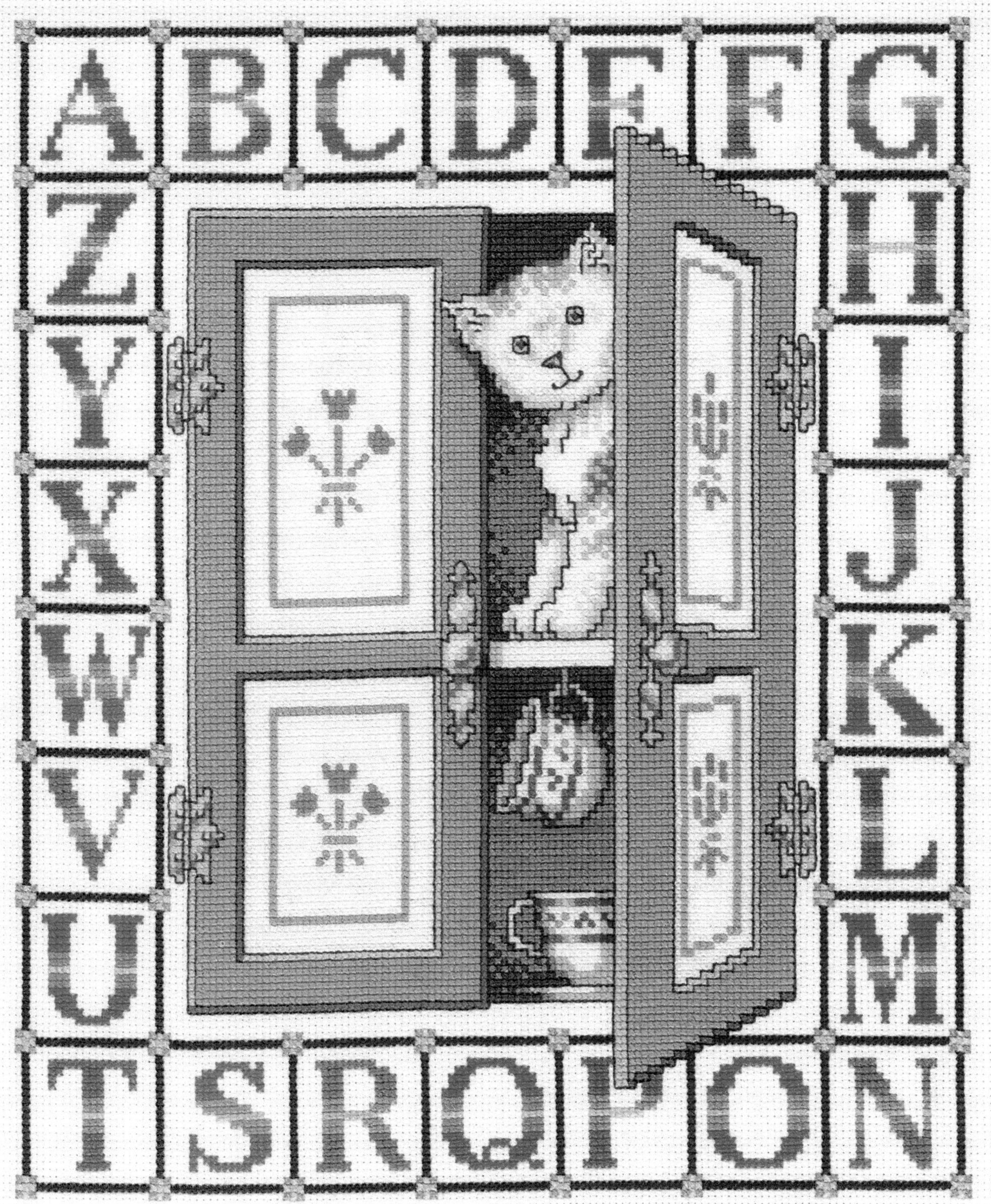

Great A, little a, bouncing B,
The cat's in the cupboard
And can't see me.

Fresh October brings the pheasant;
Then to gather nuts is pleasant.

To make your candles last for a',
You wives and maids give ear-o!
To put them out's the only way,
Says honest John Bolde'ro.

Tommy's tears and Mary's fears
Will make them old before their years.

Three little ghostesses, sitting on postesses,
Eating buttered toastesses, greasing their fistesses,
Up to their wristesses, oh, what beastesses
To make such feastesses.

Catch him, crow! Carry him, kite!
Take him away till the apples are ripe;
When they are ripe and ready to fall,
Here comes baby, apples and all!

If you are not handsome at twenty,
Not strong at thirty,
Not rich at forty,
Not wise at fifty,
You never will be.

Good night, sleep tight,
Wake up bright in the morning light,
To do what's right with all your might.

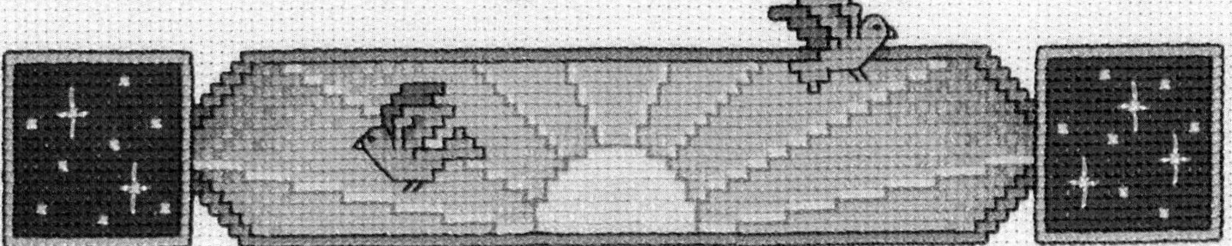

Dull November brings the blast;
Then the leaves are whirling fast.

A wise old owl sat in an oak.
The more he heard, the less he spoke;
The less he spoke, the more he heard.
Why aren't we all like that wise old bird?

Wee Willie Winkie
Runs through the town,
Upstairs, downstairs,
In his nightgown,
Rapping at the window,
Crying through the lock,
Are the children in their beds,
For now it's eight o'clock?

The boughs do shake, the bells do ring,
So merrily comes our harvest in,
Our harvest in, our harvest in,
So merrily comes our harvest in.
We've ploughed, we've sowed,
We've reaped, we've mowed,
We've got our harvest in.

Ride away, ride away,
Johnny shall ride,
He shall have a pussycat
Tied to one side;
He shall have a little dog
Tied to the other,
And Johnny shall ride
To see his grandmother.

I see
the moon and
the moon sees me.
God bless the moon
and God bless me.

Chill December brings the sleet,
Blazing fire, and Christmas treat.

Smiling girls, rosy boys,
Come and buy my little toys,
Monkeys made of gingerbread,
And sugar horses painted red.

Christmas is coming,
The geese are getting fat,
Please to put a penny
In an old man's hat.
If you haven't got a penny,
A ha'penny will do;
If you haven't got a ha'penny,
Then God bless you.

When December snows fall fast,
Marry, and true love will last.

Little Jack Horner sat in a corner,
Eating of Christmas pie;
He put in his thumb and pulled out a plum,
And said "What a good boy am I!"

Golden slumbers kiss your eyes,
Smiles awake you when you rise,
Sleep, pretty baby; do not cry,
And I will sing you a lullaby.

Of all
the sayings in the world,
The one to see you through
Is "Never trouble trouble,
Till trouble troubles you."

Mother Goose and the Sampler

Mother Goose and the traditional sampler, two of our most beloved artifacts of bygone days, have much in common: Both employed rhymes to reveal their wisdom and both began their rise in popularity at about the same time. Additionally, each had long and colorful histories before finally settling comfortably into the laps of children, whose loving embrace of Mother Goose's nonsense and wisdom helped create for the verses a prominent niche in our literary heritage. And youthful hands helped transform the sampler from a schoolroom exercise into a unique and expressive art form.

Examplars

Mention samplers today and many people think only of cross-stitch. Long ago, however, samplers or "examplars," as they were once known, displayed a variety of stitches, designs, and color combinations. Before there were printed patterns, women shared and exchanged needlework ideas, quickly copying swatches of new work before they could be forgotten. A strip of linen was reserved as a "notebook" on which designs were placed haphazardly until the cloth was filled. These samplers were highly valued, and handed down through generations. As printed pattern books became common, the practical record-keeping sampler fell into disuse. Thereafter, only the children who still required practice, stitched designs and letters on samplers.

American Samplers

Samplers already had a long and rich tradition by the time the first settlers sailed for North America in the seventeenth century. While the early American colonists took great pride in their independence of religious thought, their style and artistic taste remained decidedly English. The earliest surviving American sampler was completed by Loara Standish around the year 1645 (Fig. 1), and is indistinguishable from English samplers of that time.

From the earliest days, Massachusetts towns emphasized reading—not for educational purposes, but so people could read their Bibles. Within a century of arrival—Massachusetts Bay Colony was first settled in 1630—schools began springing up. An early Boston school for girls advertised its priorities with ". . . a Boarding School, where will be Carefully taught Flourishing, Embroidery and all sorts of Needlework, also Filigree, Painting on Glass, writing, arithmetick and singing Psalm Tunes."

Many girls (and a few boys) from four to fifteen years old worked a simple alphabet sampler at home or in a local dame school. Only well-to-do girls went on to the costly private schools or academies. There they produced elaborate samplers, adding verses, pastoral scenes, flowers, and fanciful animals to their alphabets. The finished works represented the girls' maturity and accomplishments. They were usually signed, dated, framed, and proudly displayed on the walls of the family home.

"Loara Standish is my name/Lord guide my heart that I may do thy will/And fill my hands with such convenient skill/As will conduce to virtue devoid of shame/And I will give glory to thy name."

Loara Standish, daughter of the legendary Captain Miles Standish, is considered to be the first girl to complete a sampler on American soil. The work is stylistically consistent with English samplers, many of which were brought to North America with other household belongings. Typical of the craftsmanship of the day, the front and back are mirror images of one another.

Fig. 1

(Photograph courtesy of The Pilgrim Society, Plymouth, Massachusetts.)

Throughout the eighteenth century, regional differences began to appear. New patterns were developed, often unique to an area, city, or school. Some patterns remained isolated while others gained wide popularity. Adam and Eve with the serpent, seen on Mary Emmon's sampler (Fig. 2), appeared in Boston and spread quickly to other areas. The Balch School of Providence, Rhode Island, often

"Mary Emmons Wrought this Sampler/in the Thirteen year of hir Age August 8 1749/Behold Alass Our Days We Spend/How vain they be how soon they End"

Mary Emmons's sampler is one of a distinctive group of samplers featuring the "Boston band pattern," just below the top alphabet. This band was peculiar to the Boston area and remained popular until the 1820's. Adam and Eve were also common on needlework from this area, sometimes charmingly attired in proper colonial dress.

Fig. 2

(Photograph from *American Needlework Treasures: Samplers and Silk Embroideries from the Collection of Betty Ring*. Copyright © 1987 by Betty Ring, E. P. Dutton.)

featured two trumpeting angels and an imposing floral border. The schools around Portland, Maine, usually featured verse and genealogy, along with local scenes, all surrounded by rose and vine borders. On the whole, samplers of this period displayed many distinctive styles, establishing them as uniquely American.

By the beginning of the nineteenth century, the popularity of samplers was at its peak. A school's reputation could rest almost entirely on the style, quality, and originality of the samplers its students produced. These were complex pieces, heavily influenced by the school mistresses who probably drew their own designs, thereby accounting for the similarity of samplers from any particular school. Increased emphasis on academics gave rise to map samplers and cross-stitched multiplication tables. Large depictions of the school itself, painstakingly stitched brick by brick, were not uncommon. Memorial embroideries, an outgrowth of the sampler, usually featuring a lady bent weeping by a monument beneath a willow tree, became tremendously popular after the death of George Washington. Yet even within the strictest guidelines, young girls often managed to create very personal, very expressive works of art. They portrayed their homes, families, pets, and gardens. Their youthful fantasies were embodied in florid scenes of courting couples. Occasionally the true child would shine through the most formal exercise, as did one little girl who stitched across the bottom of her Washington Memorial sampler, "Patty Polk did this and she hated every stitch she did in it. She loves to read much more."

Serious sampler work waned by the mid-nineteenth century as the country moved toward public schooling. But many decades later these classroom exercises caught the eye of collectors. For the American-schoolgirl sampler was unique. Betty Ring, the noted sampler historian and collector, writes:

> *The tolerance of child-like imperfections, particularly in lettering, made American samplers conspicuously different from English ones. The strict English schoolmistress would rarely accept such mistakes, and a girl was forced to correct her work until she arrived at perfection. Yet today, informality in design and traces of childish impatience lend charm to American samplers and convey a sense of youthful innocence more appealing than flawless execution.*

Reality, it seems, was seldom a requirement in samplers. People were often bigger than houses, dogs might be indistinguishable from cats (and cats indistinguishable from lions), and letters sometimes landed in improbable places. Rarely has any other art form captured so well the innocence and spirit of childhood.

Sampler Verses and Mother Goose

Elaborate samplers nearly always included verses, usually stressing virtue, goodness, and industry. Isaac Watts's *Divine Songs for Children* appears to have been a popular source for many needleworkers, but the Bible, Shakespeare, and other authors are represented as well. The most commonly occurring verse is religious:

> *Jesus permit thy gracious name to stand*
> *As the first efforts of an infant's hand*
> *And while her fingers o're this canvas move*
> *Engage her tender heart to seek thy love*
> *May she with thy dear children share a part*
> *And write thy name thyself upon her heart.*

The mature, often morbid themes of many verses seem incongruous with the delicate age of the child wielding needle and thread, as in this verse from a nine-year-old:

> *Cordelia L Bennet is My Name*
> *New york is My Station*
> *Heaven is my Dwelling Place*
> *and Christ is My Salvation*
> *When I am Dead and in my Grave*
> *and all my Bones are Rotten*
> *When This you See Remember me*
> *That I Be not Forgotten*

Occasionally the carefree child is glimpsed through the words, but even then the stern gaze of the mistress can be felt:

The trees were green/The sun was hot
Sometimes I worked/And sometimes not
Seven years my age/My name Jane Grey,
And often much/Too fond of play.

Here is one from the "all hands must be busy" school of thought:

This needle work of Mine doth tell
When a child is learned well
By my parents I was taught
Not to spend my time for naught.

Throughout the eighteenth century, sampler work by children kept pace with the growing popularity of printed nursery rhyme books. Yet, surprisingly, these rhymes were rarely stitched by the children who loved them. Apparently such frivolous verses were considered unfit to appear on a needlework that was meant to show the maturity and discipline of its maker. Nevertheless many of the verses in these early books and verses on the samplers appear to have had common sources. The Fleetwood–Quincy sampler (1654) displays this inscription:

In prosperity friends are plenty
In adversity not one in twenty.

Later Mother Goose tells us:

In time of prosperity, friends will be plenty
In time of adversity, not one in twenty.

An eighteenth century sampler declares:

Labor for learning before you grow old
For it is better than silver or gold

When silver is gone and money is spent
Then learning is most excellent.

Mother Goose recites a shorter version:

When land is gone and money spent
Then learning is most excellent.

In another parallel a sampler notes:

Could we with ink the Ocean fill
Were the whole earth of parchment made
Were every single stick a Quill
And every man a scribe by trade
To write the love of God above
Would drain the Ocean dry.

Says Mother Goose in an obvious parody:

If all the world were paper,
And all the sea were ink;
If all the trees were bread and cheese,
What should we have to drink?

There are other examples of verses appearing both on samplers and in Mother Goose volumes, but all of them fall into the category of proverbs or old sayings drawn from the great pool of our cultural heritage. These words of wisdom give us insight into how people lived and learned in earlier centuries. They distill hard-earned knowledge and beliefs into tiny bright gems that a child can hold and cherish and pass along to the next child.

BIBLIOGRAPHY

ALLEN, GLORIA SEAMAN. *Family Record: Genealogical Watercolors and Needlework.* Washington, D.C.: DAR Museum, 1989.

BARING-GOULD, WILLIAM S. and CEIL. *The Annotated Mother Goose.* New York: Clarkson N. Potter, 1962.

BOLTON, ETHEL STANWOOD and EVA JOHNSON COE. *American Samplers.* Boston: Massachusetts Society of the Colonial Dames of America, 1921.

CLABBURN, PAMELA. *The Needleworker's Dictionary.* London: Macmillan, 1976.

DON, SARAH. *Traditional Samplers.* New York: Viking, 1986.

FORIS, MARIA and ANDREAS. *Charted Folk Designs for Cross-stitch Embroidery,* trans. Heinz Edgar Kiewe. New York: Dover Publications, 1975.

HARBESON, GEORGIANA BROWN. *American Needlework.* New York: Coward-McCann, 1938.

HUISH, MARCUS. *Samplers and Tapestry Embroideries,* 2nd ed. London: Longmans, Green, 1913.

KASSELL, HILDA. *Stitches in Time.* New York: Duell, Sloan and Pearce, 1966.

KRUEGER, GLEE. *A Gallery of American Samplers: The Theodore H. Kapnek Collection.* New York: E.P. Dutton, 1978.

———. *New England Samplers to 1840.* Sturbridge, Mass.: Old Sturbridge Village, 1978.

RING, BETTY. *American Needlework Treasures.* New York: E.P. Dutton, 1987.

———. "The Balch School in Providence, Rhode Island," *Antiques.* Apr., 1975.

———. "Mary Balch's Newport Sampler," *Antiques.* Sept., 1983.

———. *Needlework—An Historical Survey.* New York: Universe Books, Antiques Magazine Library, 1975.

———. "Salem Female Academy," *Antiques.* Sept., 1974.

———. "Samplers and Silk Embroideries of Portland, Maine," *Antiques.* Sept., 1988.

SCHIFFER, MARGARET B. *Historical Needlework of Pennsylvania.* New York: Charles Scribner's Sons, 1958.

SEBBA, ANNE. *Samplers, Five Centuries of a Gentle Craft.* New York: Thames & Hudson, 1979.

STUDEBAKER, SUE. *Ohio Samplers: Schoolgirl Embroideries, 1803–1850.* Lebanon, Ohio: Warren County Historical Society, 1988.

SWAN, SUSAN BURROWS. *Winterthur Guide to American Needlework.* New York: Crown Publishers, Rutledge Books, 1976.

WEISSMAN, JUDITH REITER and WENDY LAVITT. *Labors of Love: America's Textiles and Needlework, 1650–1930.* New York: Alfred A. Knopf, 1987.